Welcome to our HappyStoryGarden!

Zinaida Kirko

DRAGON ISLAND

„˙I would love to help!˙ he exclaimed, ˙but what can I do…
an ordinary Yol?˙

˙Oh,˙ the Diarius waved his hand. ˙What can a simple
Yol do?

Everyone is capable of doing what he believes in… „

Chapter 1

Noble Yols

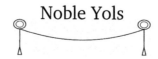

The city of the Yols was built on a huge hill. It is so big that the Yols had never been at its foot. They never ventured out of their little world and did not even know this place existed.

The Grokhan's house was one of the oldest. It has stood since the time when strangers came to the city and told fables, at which the Yols only laughed, not believing a single word. The strangers eventually became legends themselves, as did their stories. All the Yols thought so, everyone except for the Grokhans. After all, their house was one of the oldest.

The Grokhan family was small. Old man Grokhan was so old that he had not been out for many years. He was short and gnarled, with a long grey beard that reached the floor.

His daughter Ruzelda, who supported the entire household, was a sweet woman with huge eyes the colour of a rainy evening. During her free time, she made jewellery from metals. She was a very quiet woman, hardly ever saying a word all her life.

Her son Arvin, who had just turned twelve, was a short, handy little boy who did not remember a day in his life when he did not work.

Every morning, Arvin got up before everyone else and went outside. The Grokhans' house was on the very edge of a cliff. Arvin was always fond of watching the endless ocean of clouds stretching in all directions.

Behind it was the city... Arvin considered it noisy and boring. He wanted to run away and float away through the clouds. But where? What was there outside of this? Or what was down at the bottom of the cliff?

"Nobody knows..." old man Grokhan answered his questions, "but there are legends..."

And all the evenings, the old man told Arvin about the strangers and what they had said to the Yols many, many years ago.

During the day, Arvin worked long and hard - carrying bales of flour. The Yols mainly ate bread from seven hundred varieties of wheat, which they grew themselves and were very proud of.

When Arvin tried talking to them about fables or legends, they twirled their fingers to their temples and laughed.

Everyone considered the Grokhans to be strange and crazy, and the boy always got the most demanding work, which the others refused to do.

The whole day, Arvin waited for the evening to plunge into fairy tales and legends again. He imagined that a stranger would finally come to their city one day, and the boy would learn the whole truth from him.

The day Arvin turned twelve, he came home especially tired. A delicious dinner prepared by Ruzelda was waiting for him on the table, and old Grokhan had already prepared a new story for him. He cleared his throat as the boy swallowed the last bite of the bread casserole and said:

"Today, I will tell you a special story... about Dragon Island."

Arvin opened his eyes wide and prepared to listen.

"And it is special because, unlike all other stories, this one is true, and there is no doubt about it!"

"How can you be so sure?" Arvin asked.

"Oh," said the old man, "I have been saving this story for many years to tell you one day. A long time ago... when I was still very young, the Yol city was not as big as it is today, and the mist of clouds under the cliff was not so dense, my father told me a story about a Yol who fell into the sky and ended up on Dragon Island."

"But how can you fall into the sky?" Arvin asked in bewilderment.

"Who knows! Old Grokhan gestured with his hands. But my father told me - until the Yol falls into the sky, he will forever remain just a Yol. And if you want to become someone else or test legends, you need to do something incredible."

"So, that same Yol... fell into the sky and ended up on Dragon Island. How much he experienced and saw there!"

"But how did he get home? And how did others find out about his travels?"

"He returned on the back of the dragon! A real dragon... its skin was covered with golden scales, and his eyes were kind and wise. My father himself saw how this same Yol jumped to the ground from the back of a dragon!

"And what happened then?"

Old Grokhan sighed heavily.

"The Yols didn't believe him. They laughed at him until his death. So, he fell ill and died without saying a word to anyone else until his last days. But what there is certainly no doubt about is that Dragon Island exists."

Arvin could not sleep until morning. The story that old Grokhan told him did not give him peace.

"If the island really exists, why is no one looking for it?" he shook the old man by the shoulders before dawn.

"Where? What?" the old man asked, waking up and rubbing his eyes.

"Where is it? This island?" Arvin did not let up.

"Floats somewhere in the fog," grunted old Grokhan. "But I'm telling you, to find it, you need to fall into the sky..."

Arvin had been carrying bales of flour all day. Today, they seemed especially heavy to him. How could he have been doing such a useless thing when it was clear that Dragon Island was floating somewhere in the mist, in the middle of the clouds?

After work, he did not go home but decided to go to the other side of the city. There was the house of the Ikhars. They were rich, very rich. Compared to the Grokhans' house, theirs was a real palace!

The Ikhars were engineers. All new buildings in the city were made by them. It was said that there was nothing that the Ikhars could not build. They loved their work, they engaged in it with joy, and their desire for impeccability reached madness.

However, everyone in the city knew this was not what the Ikhars were actually famous for. In deep cellars, they practised alchemy and worked miracles that only they knew how to do. Precisely because of this, everyone in the city was afraid of them.

The evening was unusually still, and the dark, star-studded sky was especially clear. Arvin stopped outside the Ikhar house and hesitated. He was scared like never before in his life. The white marble columns of their house were too perfect compared to the rotten wooden stanchions of the Grokhan dwelling.

"Come in, my young friend; what are you waiting for?" he heard a calm voice.

Arvin looked up and saw a tall Yol in a green velvet suit on the balcony. The Yol smiled restrainedly and pointed to the door with his hand.

Arvin swallowed in fear but pulled himself together and took a few steps forward.

The door opened before him, and he found himself in a spacious living room. Everywhere were vases of fresh flowers, rich tapestries, and furniture of the most skilful workmanship.

The Ikhars that came out of the different rooms were beautiful and sophisticated. They surrounded the boy and led him into the living room. They all looked at him with interest.

"Who are you?" they asked calmly. "And what brought you to us at such a late hour?"

But their noble air and impeccable appearance made Arvin's mouth dry. He imagined how they would start laughing at him and could not say a word.

"He must have the wrong house," said the young woman while handing the boy a glass of water.

"No," the elder Yol objected, "I can see from his eyes that he has business with us."

"Come on," the young Yol encouraged him, "tell us, why you came to us?"

Arvin drank the water and took a very deep breath before speaking.

"I want you to build me a ship that will fall into the sky and take me to Dragon Island!" he blurted out.

The Yols exchanged glances. They did not laugh but were amazed and puzzled. They were silent for what seemed like an eternity while they all assessed in their head the reality and complexity of the task.

"We have never received such an order," the elder Yol finally said.

"So, you think it's impossible?" Arvin asked dejectedly.

"On the contrary," objected the Yol, who had been silent before, "nothing is impossible for us."

The rest of the Ikhars nodded. They looked serious and even a little worried, as if they had been challenged.

"You see," said old Ikhar, "if we do not fulfil your order, the Yols in the city will no longer consider us the greatest engineers and builders."

"However, a question remains," said the second woman. "How will you pay us for your order?"

"I will give you everything that I have accumulated over many years of work," said Arvin. He was clearly surprised by their interest.

Smiles played on the faces of the Ikhars.

"No!" The young woman shook her head, "That's not enough. You..." she thought for a moment, "will bring us the heart of a dragon."

The others nodded.

"Heart of the biggest dragon!" said the old Ikhar.

"Then everyone in the city will know that we are the strongest family clan, and all power will belong to us!"

"Yes," the rest of the Ikhars agreed. "What do you say?"

Arvin didn't know what to say. He knew nothing about dragons and could not even imagine how and for what he would harm them. However, he knew that if he didn't get to Dragon Island, his life would be meaningless, so he only nodded in response.

"Fine," Ikhars clapped their hands and began to shake hands with Arvin, "you are our most unusual client."

Arvin stood up, feeling that they had already shown him too much kindness. It was rude to take up any more of their time.

"Come to us in nine full moons, and you will receive your ship."

"Thank you," was all Arvin could say before the door of the noble house slammed shut behind him.

He ran all the way home without stopping. Having reached the house, he circled it and went out to the cloudy ocean. Clouds, illuminated by the brilliance of the stars and moons, swirled and drifted forward as far as the eye could see. And somewhere out there... beyond the horizon, a distant and mysterious... Dragon Island was waiting for him.

Chapter 2

The Inverted Ship

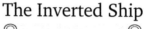

All nine moons passed unnoticed by Arvin. He said nothing to Ruzelda and old Grokhan, but only worked as hard as he could and, coming home, thought about the future.

"You have become quite taciturn lately," his grandfather told him at dinner. "As if fairy tales and legends no longer interest you."

Arvin got up and went to the window. He did not know how to lie and tried to hide his eyes from the old man. But he could keep nothing from old Grokhan.

"I know... I know you're up to something," he said. "But you don't have to tell me. Just remember that wherever you go, do not forget about the city of Yols - a city in the middle of an ocean of clouds. After all, somewhere else, you will always be just a stranger, but here..."

"What's the point?" Arvin asked, unable to stand it. "It's not for nothing that foreigners stopped coming here. Yols are not interested in anything!"

He lay down to sleep and turned away. The old man sighed.

"You want to fall into the sky," he drawled. "But can you face it? I'll tell you another tale... about the dragon's heart..."

Arvin immediately pricked up his ears, ready to listen.

"That Yol... that got to the Island of Dragons, came back for help, and he saddled the dragon for a reason," said the old man, "hmm... ahem." The old man was falling asleep.

Arvin sat up on the bed and turned to the old man to finish listening to the story, but the old man was already asleep. The boy began to shake him, but it did not help.

"Be careful," the old Yol mumbled in his sleep, "just be careful, my boy... the one who will return... must have a dragon's heart…"

Early in the morning, before dawn, Arvin woke up. He noticed a bracelet on his hand and realised that it was a gift from Ruzelda. She probably also guessed that he was going to leave the house.

For some time, the boy stood in indecision. He didn't want to leave them. Who will help his mother and grandfather? And what if something happens to him, and he can no longer return? However, dawn was drawing near.

The boy went to Ruzelda's bed and kissed her while she slept. How proud she will be of him when he returns and tells her everything he saw.

Arvin left the house with a heavy heart and went to the house of the Ikhars. He did not walk but ran through the city, past low and high houses, along roads that he knew like the back of his hand. He couldn't wait to find out as soon as possible whether the noble Yols had fulfilled their promise.

When he approached the house of the Ikhars, it became clear to him that they had succeeded. Behind the tall building, in the backyard, was something very large, covered with a rich cloth. And the Ikhars stood around, waiting for Arvin to appear.

"Here he is," said the old woman. "A brave youth of the House of Grokhan."

"Are you ready to risk everything and go on a journey for the dragon heart?" asked the old Yol.

"Because it's too late to refuse!" said the young Ikhar.

Arvin nodded in response.

The Yols removed the rich veil, and a huge ship appeared before him. However, it was not just a ship. It hung upside down in the air! The young man gasped in surprise.

"How can I manage this ship alone?!" he thought.

The Ikhars seemed to read his thoughts.

"Come on, get under it," said the old Yol, "and you will understand everything."

Arvin took a hesitant step forward, then ducked under the side of the ship and found himself on its deck. He saw two dozen wooden rowers sitting upside down at the oars. Before he even opened his mouth, they immediately set to work. Arvin seemed to be glued to the bottom of the ship, which was already rushing forward in full sail, and when he turned around, the house of Ikhar was left far behind.

Now he was rising higher and higher into the heavens on the ship. Under him, the city of Yols floated as always, immersed in the clouds. The rowers did not let up and rowed forward with a vengeance until there was nothing left around but the endless sky.

So, they sailed for days and nights, and Arvin would look down in search of land or something that would resemble the Isle of Dragons. He breathed in the fresh air of the winds passing by, and he was seized with a sense of future great discoveries. At last, the legends will come to life, he thought, and become reality. He also thought about the words of old Grokhan about not forgetting the city of Yol and decided that he would definitely return to do something significant for his people. But what could he do, a mere little Yol?

Some days later, water and provisions had almost run out, and the shore was still not visible. Arvin's confidence began to waver. He sat at the side and watched the clouds and fog. They twisted into bizarre shapes and images and reminded him either of the coast or of his own hometown, but as soon as he looked closely, they melted and dissolved in the air without leaving a trace.

14

When he had almost completely lost hope, he noticed something shining in the distance. Arvin ran up to the prow of the ship and took a closer look. Is it another mirage? Something approached him with confidence and then clumsily flopped upside down on the deck.

Arvin approached the creature. It was a small bird with bright golden feathers. It was clearly exhausted. He brought it the last remaining water and gave it a drink. The bird jumped up and looked at its saviour with fear.

"Who are you?" it suddenly spoke.

Arvin gasped in surprise but immediately remembered that he had to be polite to his new guest.

"I am Arvin," he replied, "A Yol from a city on a hill in the middle of the clouds."

The bird breathed a sigh of relief.

"Oh, Yols," it chuckled, "those who have not seen anything and know nothing!"

And then it laughed.

"That's why I have to see everything and find out everything!" Arvin said.

"And what will you do with all this knowledge?" the bird asked.

"I will create a map of the heavens so that all Yols can travel wherever and whenever they want, so that they will all know what and where everything is!"

"What noble dreams," said the bird, proudly striding along the side of the ship. "However, for many days now, you have been aimlessly ploughing the skies and to no purpose!" and it laughed again.

Arvin sighed dejectedly. He knew it was true.

"I will help you," said the bird, "if you help me."

Arvin immediately became alert.

"You see," it said, "I am a Diarius," and the bird immediately turned into a little man, so tiny that he could fit in the palm of Arvin's hand.

"I can be a bird, and I can be a man."

He smoothed his bright white long hair.

"Or I can be many birds at once. We eavesdrop on important secrets of the world in all its corners and tell whoever needs to know."

A whole flock of birds appeared in front of Arvin, which then turned back into a laughing little man.

"There are not many of us, but we all serve the noble family of Lemoires, who live on Dragon Island. I need to get there as soon as possible! Without your help, I can't do it!"

"That's exactly where I'm going," Arvin exclaimed, "but I haven't been able to find the right path for many days now."

"That's it," the little man laughed. "It's immediately clear that you are from the Yol clan. Turn the ship's steering wheel so that it falls into the sky, and very soon, you will find yourself where you need to be."

Arvin started towards the helm but suddenly stopped.

"But what awaits me on Dragon Island?" he asked.

"Oh," said the little man, "the island is stuck in an endless war. Everything was fine while the dragons were controlled by the great Uhl. However, he was betrayed and destroyed by Gregus, whom he considered his best friend. He took his power and began to command all the dragons of the island, creating evil and destruction. He instils fear not only in local inhabitants but also in all the surrounding countries, threatening to subordinate them to his will. But the worst thing is that Gregus captured the princess of the great family of Lemoires, Elma, who was supposed to become the ruler when she came of age. Now no one knows where she is. That's exactly who I'm looking for."

Arvin could not imagine that so much was happening in the world, and the Yols had never heard of it.

"I would love to help!" he exclaimed, "but what can I do... an ordinary Yol?"

"Oh," the Diarius waved his hand. "What can a simple Yol do? Everyone is capable of doing what he believes in. And if you don't believe in anything, then you can't do anything!"

He laughed.

"However, if you are not afraid, turn the steering wheel five times to the left, seven times to the right and one time towards yourself, and then get me to Dragon Island as soon as possible!"

Arvin immediately climbed on deck and turned the wheel with all his might. In the next moment, the huge ship seemed to fall into an invisible hole and then rolled over and stood the right way up. The bottom was now in its correct place as the sails stretched up into the blue sky.

"Wow," Arvin exclaimed.

In the distance, a majestic green shore was already visible, and what made it even more beautiful was that dragons were circling over it!

"Is it...?"

"Dragon Island!"

The little man finished the phrase for him and, turning into a flock of small golden birds, scattered across the sky and disappeared.

Chapter 3

Dragon Island

Wooden rowers continued to work tirelessly as the ship approached the cherished shore. Arvin's heart was beating faster. Are fairy tales and legends finally becoming reality? He was looking forward to telling the Yols when he got back and how they would consider him a hero.

As soon as the ship docked, it was immediately surrounded by creatures Arvin had never seen before. They were fat and dirty and much taller than Yols. Their shaggy heads were red and black, and their noses and ears were so ugly and large that they were quite unpleasant to look at. They were called the Ratters, a wild people that Gregus hired to control the lands he captured.

"Who are you, and why did you come?" they yelled, plunging their axes into the prow of the ship.

"Wood!" concluded the largest Ratter. "A good Beechwood, very valuable!"

"Don't touch it!" protested Arvin, "I need this ship to return home!"

The Ratters laughed and then immediately sat down as one. From somewhere above, a huge shadow crept over the land, followed by a long body covered with dark purple scales, and a minute later, a dragon landed among them. For a few moments, he dusted himself off and folded his membranous wings. Then he turned and his huge, burning amber fiery eyes dug into the boy.

"What's going on here?" he asked and fired a column of fire into the air.

The creatures fussed.

"The boy is an outlander!" they shouted to the dragon, crouching and hiding.

"Destroy him! Kill him on the spot!"

But Arvin did not hear them and was not afraid. He looked at the dragon as if spellbound, as if he had been hypnotised by his sight alone.

"Aren't you afraid of me?" the dragon asked, leaning towards Arvin.

"No," replied the boy.

The dragon laughed.

"So small and not afraid…"

He released several more pillars of fire into the air, but Arvin didn't move.

"Gregus ordered to kill rebellious foreigners on the spot," the Ratters hissed. "Are you really disobeying the Sovereign?!"

The dragon's eyes dimmed.

"He is a Yol… from the country of Yols," the Ratter suddenly shouted.

The dragon was startled upon hearing this and exhaled another pillar of fire. However, he immediately took on an impassive expression.

"Throw him in the dungeon," he said. "Gregus will surely want to see another Yol that fell into the sky!"

With that, he turned and took to the air, taking the shadow with him and bringing back the sun.

The jubilant Ratters grabbed Arvin and dragged him away. When he looked back, he saw how they split his flying ship into pieces with their axes. The young Yol cried out in despair. Now, he will never be able to tell his people about anything.

-Arvin was dragged roughly through the streets of the city. All around were outlandish looking buildings, colourful walls, roofs, cobbled streets and transparent bridges. It seemed clean and comfortable here. The young man wondered how such dirty and clumsy Ratters could create such incredible beauty. It soon became clear to him that completely different creatures were hiding behind the doors and windows of the buildings. They were slim and incredibly beautiful but they disappeared so quickly that Arvin did not have time to see them properly.

Soon, the boy was pushed inside a huge tower and led up a winding staircase that seemed to have no end. When they reached the top, the door opened and the prisoner was thrown to the floor. He found himself on a small platform overlooking the entire island.

"Very soon, you will become a dragon's dinner," the Ratters laughed, "and perhaps Gregus will decide to eat you himself as soon as he finds out who you are."

They chained him by his leg to a stone ledge and slammed the door. In disbelief, he stepped back and stumbled upon someone sleeping on the floor.

"Careful," he heard a sonorous voice. "I'm trying to sleep."

Arvin turned around and saw a creature similar to those he saw on the streets of the city. It was also chained.

"Who are you?" Arvin asked.

"Ah…," the creature drawled, "another outlander. You are all drawn to stare at the dragons… and no one realises how dangerous they are."

Arvin sighed. The creature stretched and sat down.

"I am Loy," said the prisoner, "of the people of the Lemoires."

He was thin, slender and very handsome, like all Lemoires. When he smiled, it seemed that there was no one happier in the world. Arvin felt uncomfortable because the Yols were short and strong with tassels of wool on their ears and, as it seemed to him, were not famous for their beauty.

"I am Arvin," he said and sat down on the dirty floor. "A Yol from the country of Yols."

"Wow," Loy exclaimed.

"What's the matter?" Arvin asked, offended. "Why is everyone so surprised when they find out who I am?"

"Don't you know yourself?" Loy was surprised, "Didn't Uhl tell you anything?"

"Uhl?"

Arvin remembered how the bird-man, Diarius, had mentioned him but had no idea who Uhl really was.

"Uhl was a Yol!" said Loy. "Didn't you know?"

Arvin sighed. He would know if the other Yols knew how to listen and believe and not just laugh at strangers.

"Tell me everything you know!" he demanded impatiently.

Loy settled himself comfortably and began his story.

"Once upon a time, we, Lemoires, ruled this island, and dragons lived their lives, constantly devastating our cities and villages, eating livestock and burning fields. And we had no salvation from them because the dragons considered themselves much smarter and stronger than us. But, one day, a young Yol named Uhl arrived on our island. They say he looked just like you! And when he found out about our trouble, he immediately promised to help us! So, Uhl disappeared, and exactly ten days later, he returned and..."

Loy fell silent, stretching and yawning.

"Well, go on!" Arvin demanded impatiently.

"So… when Uhl returned," Loy continued, "all the dragons… a miracle, I would say… all the dragons began to obey him!"

"How so?" Arvin was surprised.

"I'm telling you! He arrived on the island and said: 'Dragons of the island, come to me!' and all the dragons immediately flocked to him... hundreds... thousands of dragons began to listen to him. And he said: 'You will no longer ruin or destroy cities, but you will help the noble people of the Lemoires and protect them from now on and always!'. And the dragons agreed! How the Lemoires rejoiced!"

"What happened next?" Arvin asked.

"Hmm ... I'll tell you," Loy stood up and walked along the roof's edge, looking in the distance. "Uhl had a friend from unknown lands named Gregus, whom he brought with him. So Gregus became jealous of him. All because both of them fell in love with Maya, the daughter of the king of the Lemoires. She chose the clumsy Yol over the handsome Gregus."

Loy laughed, but Arvin didn't see anything funny about it.

"What happened next?" he asked.

"Gregus found out that the dragons obey Uhl because he possessed a thing unknown to anyone..."

Arvin widened his eyes in surprise.

"Sunstone," Loy whispered as if it was a big secret. "They say it glows brighter than a thousand suns, and dragons are ready to do everything for its owner!"

"But where did he get it?" Arvin asked in disbelief.

"It is you who should tell me because you are also a Yol from the city of Yols in the middle of the clouds!"

And he laughed again.

"Tell me more," Arvin asked.

"So," the Lemoir continued, "Gregus stole the sunstone from Uhl! He then does everything to take away power from the Lemoires and win the heart of Maya, but she refuses to marry him and flees with Uhl. And then Gregus ordered the dragons to destroy them both."

"But after all, Uhl returned to the city of Yols alive and unharmed," interjected Arvin. "My grandfather told me!"

Loy nodded his head in agreement.

"When the dragons sent thousands of pillars of fire at them, Maya died on the spot, and Uhl... their fire did not touch him! Moreover, one of the dragons, his most faithful friend, picked him up and carried him to the skies... Since then, no one has ever seen him, and the island is ruled by Gregus, who, thanks to the stone, does not age and captures more and more lands..."

"Who is Elma?" Arvin asked.

"Mmm... someone already told you about her," Loy said with sadness in his voice. "Elma is a princess of a noble family of Lemoires, heir to the throne. Gregus keeps her imprisoned so that all the Lemoires obey him because they would rather die than obey such a ruler."

A tear ran down Loy's cheek.

"Why are you crying?" Arvin asked.

"I'm crying," answered Loy, "because Elma is my sister. Gregus practically destroyed our entire noble family."

Arvin couldn't believe what he was hearing.

"So, you are the brother of the heir to the throne of the Lemoires?"

"Yes," Loy replied, sadly looking at the vastness of the island opening from the platform, "but, alas, I will never see my sister again... except perhaps..."

He turned to Arvin.

"What?" he asked.

"You're a Yol!" said Loy, "A brave, strong and powerful Yol, the same as Uhl! You must help us!"

"No," Arvin drawled. "I'm just an unremarkable loader of flour, and I'm hardly capable of such a thing!"

"Hahaha," Loy laughed. "I know how you proudly stood and looked into the dragon's eyes without fear! I wouldn't be able to! Nobody could! Therefore, you must help us!"

Arvin thought, remembering Diarius's words about believing in himself, and decided to give it a try.

"Alright," he said firmly and stood up. "We have to get out of here as soon as possible! We must save your sister and restore justice!"

The Lemoir's eyes lit up.

"I knew it!" he shouted. "You will become even greater than Uhl!"

"Hush," Arvin put his finger to his lips. "The guards can hear. How can we get out of here?"

"No one has climbed out of this tower yet!" Loy said in a whisper. "I have been here for a long time, and I know that everyone who got here did not deserve it, but sooner or later, they all become a dragon's dinner. And I, since I am of a noble family, will be held here as a hostage until the day I die."

"We'll get out of here no matter what!" Arvin assured him.

Loy wiped away his tears and smiled hopefully.

"I knew that one day, another Yol would come to this island and save us!"

Arvin paced around the rooftop all day, jingling his chain. He examined every corner, and Loy watched him, trying not to interfere.

Finally, the boy sat down on the cold floor and bowed his head in his hands. He had to do something to get out of the tower. After all, Loy believed in him. Now, simply returning to the city of Yol would not be enough. He had already imagined how he would save Elma, take the sunstone from Gregus, and restore justice to the island. And although all this seemed impossible, he had to try.

Arvin rubbed his forehead with his hand and cried out in pain. The bracelet on his arm pricked him painfully. A gift from Ruzelda. He never had time to look at it properly. But now... he twisted the bracelet in his hands... it began to seem to him that there was something special about it.

The boy stretched it, and the bracelet turned into a key. Arvin always knew that his mother was not an ordinary woman. Even though she was silent all the time, Ruzelda was very smart and resourceful. Now, he realised that the gift she made for him had magical properties.

He inserted the key into the chain's lock and twisted. It creaked, and Arvin became free.

Loy almost screamed with joy but immediately covered his mouth with his hand. Yol set him free too.

"What should we do next?" Loy asked, rubbing his stiff legs.

Sunset was approaching, and the sky was ablaze with bright colours.

"Let's wait for darkness," said Arvin, "and then we'll try to go down."

"We can't do it just by ourselves," Loy said.

He then quietly started to sing a song.

Yol listened. He had never heard anything like it. Soon he realised that this song had a purpose. As he approached the edge of the roof, he saw that a vine was slowly creeping up towards them from below. When it reached the edge, it stopped, offering them juicy bunches of grapes. Loy immediately began to feast on them, smiling as his new friend looked at him in bewilderment.

"Lemoires have many talents," Loy said, holding out a bunch of grapes to Arvin. "Among other things, they know how to talk to plants. Meet Klaus," he stroked the vine, "He came here to help us."

Arvin happily ate the grapes, and when it got dark, they both climbed down the vine. It was not difficult for them to pass by the sleeping Ratters.

"We must get to the Water Gardens," said Loy. "Only there we can hide from the dragons who will be looking for us in the morning."

"Water Gardens?" Arvin was surprised.

"There are many things in this world that you Yols have never heard of," Loy said proudly, "but these gardens are very dangerous. No one in their right mind goes there. I'm not sure I have the courage either."

"We have no other choice," Arvin said and moved on.

All night until dawn, Arvin and Loy made their way to the gardens. But no sooner had they reached them, then the first rays of sunlight glinted on the dry ground they were walking on.

"We need to hurry," Loy said worriedly, looking at the sky. "The dragons are about to catch up with us, and there are is only wasteland here with nowhere to hide."

As soon as he said that, three huge black shadows appeared on the horizon.

"Dragons!" Arvin exclaimed.

And they, together with Loy, began to run with all their might.

"The gardens are close," Loy said, pointing to the tall mirrored pillars ahead.

Suddenly, one of the dragons landed in front of them, and they stopped in their tracks. The gardens were only a few steps away. The dragon was dark red with huge green eyes.

"So... so... so," he said and spread his wings. "Did you really think you could run away from us?"

Two other dragons, blue and black-green, landed nearby.

Loy fearfully hid behind Arvin, who, with his hands on his hips, looked defiantly at the dragons.

"We are looking for Gregus," said Arvin, "to overthrow him and free the Lemoir people!"

The dragons laughed.

"In order to overthrow Gregus, you insignificant little Yol, you must defeat thousands of dragons," the green dragon said, "and it's not as easy as you think. Do you know why?"

Arvin shook his head.

"In addition to the fact that we are all able to incinerate you with one breath," said the blue dragon," each of us possesses a force so powerful that not a single person can overcome it."

"Take me, for example," said the blue dragon, " I have the power of sadness."

He exhaled a column of fire, and Loy and Arvin felt a deep sadness. It was so strong that their hands became heavy, and they didn't want to keep moving on.

"What do we do?" Loy whispered timidly behind Arvin's back.

"I am," said the black-green dragon, "the power of fear."

He exhaled a column of fire, and the young people experienced incomparable horror.

"Nooooo," Loy drawled, then fell to the ground, unconscious.

The dragons laughed, spreading their wings and throwing their heads back.

"And I...," said the red dragon, "am the power of anger."

He sucked in as much air as he could into his chest and exhaled it all at once.

And at that moment, Arvin felt a strong protest against all the injustice experienced by the Lemoires on the island and the Yols, who lived in ignorance. He stood up and shouted so loudly that the dragons fell silent:

"You can't beat us!"

A pillar of light erupted from Ruzelda's bracelet, so bright it blinded the dragons. Arvin grabbed Loy and ran forward so fast that he reached the Water Gardens almost instantly. The dragons immediately rushed after them, but it was too late. They had both reached safety in the gardens.

Chapter 4

Water Gardens

Arvin took a breath. And when Loy came to his senses, he told him what had happened.

"How cleverly you caught them by surprise!" Loy said with a happy smile as he watched the dragons soar above them. "However, I can't believe we're in the gardens."

He trembled as he looked around.

Arvin thought about how strong the dragons were and how far more dangerous they were than he had imagined. He needed to find a way to defeat them all. He needed the sunstone. But how could he get it, a simple Yol?

Arvin stared at the tall, outlandish plants, covered from base to top with a thick layer of water. They intertwined and curled high up, creating a bizarre water jungle, and the paths between them converged and diverged, forming patterns and confusing anyone who tried to find their way.

"How big are these gardens?" he asked and moved forward.

"Some say they are endless," Loy replied, following him.

Suddenly, Arvin stopped and extended his hand towards one of the plants. He heard a slight whisper as if it was trying to tell him something.

"Don't touch it," Loy warned him. "Everything in these gardens is dangerous! Few have ever made it out alive."

Arvin withdrew his hand.

"But you know how to talk to plants," he remembered. "Ask them how we can get out."

Loy turned pale.

"These are not simple plants," he said. "They are dangerous, and I... I'm afraid!"

"Well," said Arvin, "then I'll do it."

He held out his hand, but Loy stopped him.

"You are a Yol who did not arrive on this island by chance," he said, "and you must fulfil your destiny at all costs!" he added with a more serious tone.

With these words, Loy closed his eyes and touched one of the plants.

In the next moment, he was covered with a thick layer of water and disappeared, leaving behind only splashes that scattered across the sky.

"Noooo!" shouted Arvin. "Loooy!" he called him. "Looooy!"

But there was no answer.

Arvin felt so alone and so defenceless that it seemed to him that he was in vain imagining the great things that Loy had inspired him to do and realising he was not actually capable of doing anything.

In desperation, he moved forward along whatever paths that lay ahead. Suddenly, the ground parted beneath him, and he fell into a deep hole.

He flew down for a long time and around were the roots of plants also intertwining and winding in the water column. Arvin didn't care. He understood that this was the end of his journey.

He had already said goodbye to old Grokhan, Ruzelda, and the city of Yol, which, as it now seemed to him, he had always underestimated and did not love enough. So he flew for a long time until finally he fell into the water.

He slowly sank to the bottom, watching how huge burning eyes, many eyes, were swimming around him in the darkness. Whose they were, he did not know. He just watched as they flickered everywhere, looking at him with curiosity.

Suddenly, among the roots, he saw Loy. His friend hung unconscious, entwined with plants.

"Looooy!" shouted Arvin, "Loooy!"

But bubbles of air floated out of his mouth without a sound.

More time passed. He kept sinking deeper and deeper. And when hope had already left him, Arvin felt himself move into a massive air bubble, which parted, pulled him in and closed back.

"Aaaah!" the boy shouted, rushing down at speed and hitting the ground painfully.

He got up and looked around. It was a large underwater city. Its inhabitants slowly got out of the houses and surrounded Arvin. They were small, as tall as his knee, with huge eyes and antennae-like moustaches on which wisps of light hung, cutting through the darkness.

"Yol...," they whispered, "another Yol..."

Then, an elder came out to him.

"Greetings, Yol," he said, "rarely has anyone reached our dwelling down here. Tell me, why did you come?"

The elder slowly wandered deeper into the city, calling for Arvin to follow him.

"Firstly," said the Yol, "help me rescue my friend. Secondly, help us get out of the Water Gardens. Thirdly..." he hesitated, "I don't know if you can help me with this... but I have to get the sunstone to defeat Gregus."

"Hmmm...," the elder said, "you see... nothing is ever free."

He led Arvin into a huge domed building with water everywhere. It hung in the air, on the walls and even on the ceiling. With one movement of his hand, the elder twisted it into whirlwinds and then drove it away from him to the sides. The same little creatures were everywhere. Finally, he sat down near a small lake and invited the Yol to sit beside him.

"We, the inhabitants of the Water Gardens, are memory hunters," the elder said. "To get everything you want, you must sacrifice something."

"How?" Arvin asked.

"Well," said the elder, "to free your friend, you must give me one memory from your past. The best memory."

Arvin wondered if it was easy to do.

"Okay," he said happily. "I'm ready."

He remembered how once, at the feast of flour, the Yols praised him for his hard work, and it seemed to him that the whole city was proud of him, especially old Grokhan and Ruzelda.

What a happy day it was!

But suddenly, that memory melted and disappeared, and he couldn't remember what it was about. What was it? Arvin tried to remember, but he couldn't.

Loy appeared in front of him.

"Don't trust them!" he shouted. "Do not believe a single word they say! Do not believe it!"

But he was already being carried away by the currents of water.

Arvin stood up, following him. But the elder stopped him.

"I have fulfilled my promise," he said, "but you have not yet fulfilled all your desires."

"But what about my friend?" Arvin asked.

"As I promised," the elder said, "he made it out of the gardens unharmed. But you… you wanted to defeat Gregus, didn't you? And wield the power to conquer dragons?"

It was true. Without that, Arvin couldn't just leave, so he sat down next to the elder again.

"Well," he said. "For such help, you must give me all your good memories of your whole life."

Arvin gave it some serious thought for a moment. Remembering Loy's words, he still hesitated. But why does he need happy memories? After all, they are in the past, which means they are no longer needed. But in return, he will get everything he dreamed of.

"I agree," he said at last.

"Fine," the elder smiled. "I can't give you a sunstone. Only you yourself can master it and subdue the dragons. But, alas, without good memories, you are unlikely to succeed!"

In the next moment, Arvin felt like someone had taken all the joy out of his life. There were only sad, dark memories in his head, and he no longer wanted anything.

"Do you think Gregus has always been evil? We made him this way!" the elder laughed.

But Arvin no longer remembered why he had to control the dragons and defeat Gregus. There was only sadness and emptiness in his heart.

The memory hunters left the building, taking the last wisps of light with them. Arvin was left alone in front of the shimmering pool of water, not knowing who he was or why he was there.

Chapter 5

Gregus - the Villain

Loy opened his eyes and looked around. He was on the other side of the gardens. But how did he get there?

For a few moments, he struggled to remember.

"Oh no!" he exclaimed when his memory returned to him. "My brave friend Arvin! How can I get you out of there?!"

Overcoming his fear, he immediately rushed back to the gardens, but they did not let him in, throwing him back to the ground. The plants whispered and merged into one long bush from which there was no exit or entrance.

And the dragons were already approaching from the sky. They grabbed Loy and carried him away. He flew over the island for a long time, desperately trying to free himself, but the dragons had an iron-like grip.

As soon as they approached a huge castle, a dragon let him drop safely to the ground. When Loy got up, he was surrounded by many different dragons. Also, the Ratters crowded nearby and laughed at him. As they approached, Loy thought they wanted to tear him apart, but instead, they pushed him through the gate into the throne room.

Once inside, Loy looked up and saw Gregus himself sitting on the throne. He was old, scary, tall, and hunchbacked. His eyes were black and full of caustic anger, as if he had never seen anything joyful in his life.

On his chest hung a sunstone shimmering with all colours. He sat on a large throne, and the Ratters brought him food and drink in order to please their master.

"Bring him to me," Gregus barked.

The Ratters immediately seized Loy and threw him at the feet of the sovereign.

"Come on," he croaked, moving his twisted fingers, "tell me what kind of Yol has arrived in our land and what happened to him?

"I won't say a word to you," Loy said softly.

He trembled with fear but held on with all his might to not betray his friend.

"Well," Gregus drawled with a nasty smile, "I'll get everything I need from you myself."

He touched the sunstone and waved his hand. A white dragon immediately flew to him and bowed his head.

"Do you know who it is?" Gregus said to Loy. "This is the dragon of truth... and he will make you tell me everything."

The dragon released a pillar of fire, and Loy immediately, against his will, told Gregus about everything. He immediately repented of this, but it was too late.

"Hmm... hmm," grunted Gregus and stood up, "that means the boy wanted to overthrow me! How fortunate he was captured by memory hunters... they made him think like me, and I need a successor!"

"No!" Loy exclaimed. "You don't know Arvin. He will never be like you and will never do evil as you do!"

But the ruler waved his hand, and Loy was taken away. He was thrown into a dungeon on the lowest floor of the castle, where it was damp and lonely.

The Ratters immediately seized Loy and threw him at the feet of the sovereign.

"Come on," he croaked, moving his twisted fingers, "tell me what kind of Yol has arrived in our land and what happened to him?

"I won't say a word to you," Loy said softly.

He trembled with fear but held on with all his might to not betray his friend.

"Well," Gregus drawled with a nasty smile, "I'll get everything I need from you myself."

He touched the sunstone and waved his hand. A white dragon immediately flew to him and bowed his head.

"Do you know who it is?" Gregus said to Loy. "This is the dragon of truth... and he will make you tell me everything."

The dragon released a pillar of fire, and Loy immediately, against his will, told Gregus about everything. He immediately repented of this, but it was too late.

"Hmm… hmm," grunted Gregus and stood up, "that means the boy wanted to overthrow me! How fortunate he was captured by memory hunters… they made him think like me, and I need a successor!"

"No!" Loy exclaimed. "You don't know Arvin. He will never be like you and will never do evil as you do!"

But the ruler waved his hand, and Loy was taken away. He was thrown into a dungeon on the lowest floor of the castle, where it was damp and lonely.

"I will give my last good memory," he said, "but the boy must live up to my expectations!"

The old woman fell into a trance again and then withdrew.

43

At this time, Arvin was sleeping in a deep sleep, which was suddenly broken by a quiet voice.

"Arvin, Arvin, wake up!"

He opened his eyes, and before him, in the streams of water, many eyes appeared. However, there was so much darkness and sadness in his heart that he only turned away. Suddenly, someone forcefully pulled him into the water stream, and Arvin was again in the water column, surrounded by countless eyes. They began to take on the shape of water creatures that Arvin had never seen before.

"You must wake up, Arvin!" they insisted. "Gregus wants you to learn everything he knows and become even more powerful than him. For this, he gave the most valuable thing he had."

The thought of power woke Arvin. He remembered who he was and that he must subdue the dragons.

"Who are you?" he asked angrily.

"We are beings of knowledge," they replied, "and we have the power to subjugate any feelings and emotions. Each dragon is a force, both good and bad. You can master the dragon only if you master all the forces within yourself to perfection."

Many illusory dragons immediately appeared before Arvin, and the boy saw how powerful they were.

"Come on," said the beings of knowledge, "master your sadness, anger, and greed, and you will command them!"

Arvin tried to do this for a long time. He ordered the dragons, but they did not listen.

However, the more he tried, the more he succeeded. It was easy for him to master the dark emotions and fears because they overwhelmed his heart.

Soon, he already felt how power and might were within his grasp. He was still unable to subdue the light forces of joy, happiness, and love because he had none left, and this angered him so much that even the beings of knowledge began to fear him.

Having fulfilled their part of the contract, they released him from the gardens to freedom.

At this time, Loy was in prison. In desperation, he remembered Gregus' words that his friend would now become a villain too. He was terrified, but he was also inspired by the memories of how Arvin boldly looked the dragons in the eyes and overcame all obstacles in his path. He knew that he had to do something, but it seemed to him that he would never be able to get out of the dungeon.

Suddenly, something fluttered rapidly through the window, made a circle under the ceiling and stopped right in front of him. It was a bird that immediately turned into a little man.

"Diarius!" Loy exclaimed happily.

The last time he saw the birdman was when he was a child, and he knew that they served the noble people of the Lemoires.

"Yes, it's me." said the little man. "I was sent by your sister Elma, who heard rumours that you ended up in the same castle where she was also imprisoned. I'll help you get out. And you will have to get to the top floor and free her."

Loy shuddered in fear but immediately pulled himself together. He knew he couldn't be afraid anymore. The lives of his friends depended on it.

Diarius turned into many birds. They flew around the dungeon and watched the guards, eavesdropped on their conversations, and then, seeing the key, quietly pulled it out of the lock and brought it to Loy.

"They say that Ratters are planning a feast near the castle," said Diarius, "and all the guards will be there. At that time, you and your sister must escape."

With these words, he fluttered out of the dungeon and disappeared.

Loy did just that. He waited until the corridors were empty and opened the door. He remembered how he had been in this castle a long time ago. Following his memory, he quickly found his way to the tower where his sister was.

And now, when he was close to the goal, he was noticed by one of the guards. He began to scream and call for help, but Loy sang his quiet song, and the flowers from the pots on the floor began to grow. They twisted around the Ratter and covered its mouth. Loy used the key that the Diarius had given him and freed his sister.

How happy they were to see each other because they had been apart for many years.

"You have grown taller and prettier, sister Elma!" Loy hugged her.

"How brave you have become, my dear brother Loy," she exclaimed.

"All this thanks to my friend Yol from the city in the clouds!" he answered and told her about him.

The screams of the Ratters were heard below, and they rushed to escape from the castle. They descended the winding stairs and tried to avoid being seen by anyone. Loy and Elma knew the castle well and all its secret passages and exits. But as soon as they got outside, they were surrounded by dragons.

"Where are you going?" one of them asked.

"Let us go!" Elma begged. "Aren't you tired of being oppressed by Gregus?! Don't you want freedom like it used to be?"

The dragons thought for a moment, and their eyes gradually saddened.

"As long as Lord Gregus possesses the sunstone, neither we nor you will see freedom!"

With those words, the azure dragon exhaled a pillar of fire. Elma and Loy felt suddenly sleepy. The dragons grabbed them and carried them back to the castle.

How angry Gregus was when he discovered they were trying to escape. He chained them both to a pillar in front of the castle, where a crowd of Ratters had already gathered.

"What bad timing you have chosen to run away," he said, rubbing his hands, "because I have prepared a surprise for you."

The Ratters parted, and Arvin stepped out of the crowd. Loy gasped when he saw how he had changed. His eyes were black and angry. Not a drop of former kindness and hope remained in them. And his insecurity vanished as if it had never existed.

"Hahaha," Gregus laughed, "show me, my young friend, what you can do!"

"Yes, my lord," Arvin answered, raising his hands to the sky.

Hundreds of dragons immediately flocked to him and bowed their heads.

"Now he can control them even without the sunstone," Gregus said, still laughing, "and together, we will do many terrible things!"

Loy and Elma noticed that every dragon obeyed Arvin. A few sadly stepped back instead. Those were dragons of the forces of light.

Gregus and the Ratters cheered while Arvin dutifully waited for his instructions. And the hope for a bright future faded away in the hearts of Loy and Elma.

"Let these two live until the morning to say goodbye to each other," said Gregus, "and then Arvin himself will order the dragons to eat them for breakfast."

Chapter 6

Fairies of the magic forest

Evening came. The Ratters dispersed, and Gregus retired. Arvin was taken to the castle to understand the ruler's plans, in which he was to take part. And the noble Lemoires remained alone, tied to a pole.

"What should we do, sister?" Loy asked in despair.

Elma started to think.

"I have only one friend left in the whole world," she said and quietly called him. "Diarius! Diarius!"

The man immediately appeared next to her.

"How sorry I am, mistress, that you did not manage to escape," he said sadly and guiltily, "and that I could not help you! And most of all, I grieve that it was I who brought the Yol to the island."

"You are not to blame for this," Elma answered softly. "You have done a lot for me, and I am grateful to you for that. But perhaps you could help us one more time?"

"Of course," the little man answered readily. "What should I do?"

"Go to the forest fairies, eavesdrop on their conversations and find out how we can awaken the goodness in our friend Arvin again. But hurry, time is running out!"

"It will be done," Diarius answered.

And, although this matter seemed hopeless to him, he turned into a flock of small birds and scattered across the sky.

Diarius raced towards the magical forest as fast as he could. He knew he had to remain unnoticed because the forest fairies were constantly at odds with the Diarius kind, and both peoples avoided each other. Although he had never seen them, he had heard that the fairies were moody and never did what they were told.

The little man approached the forest and sat down on one of the tall plants. He listened. The forest was asleep. The trees rustled in the wind and seemed to breathe. The inhabitants of the forest were going to bed. But not the fairies.

When Diarius approached their settlement in the middle of a forest, he saw they were in the midst of some fun and enjoyment. The fairies were beautiful and shone with magical happiness. They laughed, danced and scattered magic dust around, which flew like fireworks across the sky. Diarius saw them for the first time and could not understand how animosity could arise with such beautiful creatures.

"What are they celebrating?" the little man asked himself and flew closer.

He soon found out that it was a celebration of the coronation of the new fairy queen. He saw her, and she seemed to him to be the most beautiful creature he had ever seen in his life. Why were they so filled with hostility, he kept asking himself without finding an answer.

Suddenly, fairy dust hit him. Diarius tried to brush himself off, but it was too late. He seemed to plunge into the ocean of endless happiness, where it seemed there was neither past nor future. He immediately forgot about the noble Lemoires, who were in trouble. Forgetting everything, he fluttered into the centre of the fun and started dancing to the music.

The fairies immediately screamed, grabbed the little man, and tied him with magic threads. The music and the party stopped.

"Diarius!" they shouted, "Diarius!"

The queen flew up to him. She looked fragile, but there was an unbending will in her eyes.

"Why did you enter our kingdom?" she asked.

Intoxicated by their magic, Diarius broke into a smile.

"I came," he answered, "to say that you are the most beautiful thing I have seen in the world!"

The queen smiled indulgently. However, the fairies doused the little man with cold water, and the memory began to return to him. He told them why he had come, to plead for help.

"Why should we help you, the Diarius? Your people have always been hateful to us, and you serve some Lemoires?" the fairy said with pride. "We, fairies, do not serve anyone!"

"Yes," said Diarius, "my people have always avoided you, but now I see that it was wrong because you embody light and goodness! Besides, this is the first day of your reign, queen, and why don't you begin with something as beautiful as helping both the Diarius and Lemoires? Let this be the beginning of a friendship between our people!

The fairy paused for a moment. She had never seen a Diarius before, and this little man seemed interesting to her. She also couldn't remember what started their feud.

"Why should we help him?" the fairies around screamed.

"We don't need to be friends with anyone! Especially with Diarius! We are good on our own!"

The queen listened to their cries and stamped her foot.

"It's decided! We won't help you!" she concluded.

Diarius lowered his head.

"Although," the queen turned to the others, "if Diarius overtakes the fastest of our fairies, perhaps we should change our minds."

The fairies swirled around happily and clapped their hands. The music started playing, and the fun continued.

The fairies laughed. Diarius' mood sank even further because he knew that they were the fastest creatures in the world, and no one had yet been able to overtake them.

The little man was released and taken to the forest. One of the fairies appeared in front of him, the fastest of them all. She laughed, promising to overtake him within a count of two.

"The first one to circle the entire forest will win and receive a reward!" the queen announced and clapped her hands.

There was a signal. The poor Diarius had only just managed to turn into a bird when his rival had already disappeared from sight. Having flown a small part of the forest, he stopped by the lake and sat on the ground to catch his breath. He knew it was impossible to outrun the fairies, yet he tried his best to help his friends. A tear rolled down his cheek.

Suddenly, a fairy child appeared in front of him. She giggled and made faces at him but stopped when she saw him crying.

"This is for you from the queen," she said, handing him a small package, then flew off.

Diarius opened it. Inside was a vial of fairy dust with the inscription:

To Diarius, lover of fairies, from the queen. Let this be the first step towards the friendship of our people.

The little man was surprised but smiled and swallowed it.

In the next moment, he felt an incredible surge of strength. He immediately took off into the air and rushed as fast as any fairy had ever managed. In two counts, he had circled the entire forest three times and stopped at the feet of the queen, and his fairy rival had yet to appear.

The fairies cheered, laughed, and clapped their hands!

"Diarius won!" they shouted. "How we underestimated the Diarius! He deserves an award!"

They demanded that the queen reward him.

"Well," she said. "For your victory, you deserve that we help your friends!"

The queen and the rest of the fairies whirled in the air and then sat down in a circle. They fell silent. At that moment, the wind died down, the rustling of the leaves stopped, and the forest became so quiet as if someone had taken away all the sounds of the forest at once.

Diarius was afraid to breathe so as not to spoil their unity. He watched as the fairies began to shimmer in the most beautiful colours he had ever seen in his life. And then it stopped, and they laughed again and started dancing.

"We did what you asked," said the queen. "We asked the ancestral spirits to help your friends; the rest does not depend on us. Go home and tell your people about the power of the fairies and how they helped you!"

"Thank you, queen," said Diarius. "I will never forget what you have done for me."

She just smiled cunningly and disappeared.

At this time, Arvin slept soundly in the castle. He seemed to have fallen into an endless darkness from which there was no way out. Now and then, sad images of the past arose in his imagination. He tossed and turned, tormented in his sleep when suddenly a Yol appeared in his mind's eye. He was older than Arvin, and his eyes shone with wisdom and kindness, which seemed strange and unfamiliar to the young man.

"Hello Arvin," said the Yol. "How glad I am to see you."

"Who are you?" the boy asked with dislike.

"I am Uhl," answered the Yol. "The same Yol who took out the sunstone from the skies."

"I don't know anything about you and don't want to know," Arvin replied.

"Arvin, Arvin," Uhl said softly. "How could you forget the city of Yols amid the clouds? The smell of seven hundred varieties of wheat and freshly baked bread, the fresh breeze in the clouds in the morning, and the silent smile of Ruzelda?"

"Ruzelda?" Arvin raised his hand, looking at the bracelet, but couldn't remember where he got it.

"And the legends of old Grokhan?" continued Uhl. "And how happy were you when you won at the feast of flour?"

Arvin tried to remember. All this seemed so hidden deep in his memory that it was unattainable.

"I have come to remind you of all this," said Uhl, "and of your noble aspirations. After all, you wanted to go beyond the clouds for a reason… you wanted to fall into the sky to become more than just a Yol…"

Suddenly, a light awakened in Arvin's soul. At first, it was like a small flame, but then it grew, filling his entire being. Then, all the beautiful memories, one after another, came back to him. He lived through each one of them again, and they filled him with light and power.

"I remember everything!" he exclaimed. "I remember joy and kindness and happiness!"

Uhl smiled.

"There is little time left before dawn, my friend," he said. "So, I will tell you about the most important thing."

Arvin prepared to listen attentively, and his eyes filled with light and joy.

"You have perfectly learned to manage your dark feelings and emotions; now do the same with the light ones so that no one can ever take them away!"

"But how can I do this... a mere Yol?" Arvin asked.

His self-doubt was returning too.

Uhl shook his head and smiled.

"To defeat Gregus and learn to control all the dragons, you must defeat the last dragon... and believe... that you have a dragon heart! A Yol with a dragon heart can perform miracles! But only you can do it. Hurry up, there is not much time left!"

With these words, Uhl slowly began to dissolve. In his place, a giant grey dragon appeared. He exhaled a pillar of fire, and Arvin felt insecure like he'd never experienced before.

However, he remembered Uhl's words and those of all his friends and screamed as loudly as he could.

Then he raised his hands to the sky and subdued the dragon, who bowed his head.

Arvin felt his body fill with confidence. Feeling it, he woke up.

Ratters brought him food and drink.

"Lord Gregus is waiting for you," they said, "to execute the disobedient Lemoires!"

Refusing to eat, Arvin got up and went out to the square, where his friend Loy was tied up. Next to him was a girl of incredible beauty. When he saw her, he realised that it was Elma.

The Ratters crowded around. And the dragons circled above them and waited for the execution to begin. Gregus sat on his throne.

"Here he is, my dear Yol," he grunted when he saw the boy. "Are you ready to destroy your friends?"

"I won't do it," Arvin said firmly.

Loy and Elma looked at each other happily, and hope lit up in their eyes. The Ratters whispered.

"Then, I'll do it myself!" Gregus barked. "And then I'll destroy you too!"

He stood up and raised his hands to the sky.

"Dragons!" he ordered. "Destroy the Lemoires and this rebellious Yol!"

But the dragons didn't move. Only a single bronze dragon rose into the air and landed in front of him. It was the dragon of justice.

"For a long time, you ruled us," it said. "And ruled cruelly and mercilessly, oppressing us, as we once oppressed the people of the Lemoires. Now your reign is over, and we have a new master!"

"How?!" Gregus wondered. "How dare you disobey me?!"

Gregus grabbed the sunstone, but it didn't help him. The dragons surrounded the old lord, ready to incinerate him.

"Wait," said Arvin, "without his power, he's just a feeble old man."

With these words, he plucked the sunstone from his neck.

"Get out and never return to Dragon Island again!" Arvin ordered.

Cursing everyone, Gregus headed out of the castle.

The Ratters stood there, not knowing what to do.

"From now on, this land will be ruled with peace and justice," Arvin told them. "You will treat the Lemoires respectfully, just as they will treat you."

The Ratters bowed. Arvin freed his friends, next to whom the Diarius soared happily. The dragons surrounded their new master.

"Well," they said, "now you can command us, and whoever receives the sunstone will have the same power. We hope you use your power wisely."

Arvin thought for a moment.

"I have decided," he said at last, "that I will free you! You have been under the yoke of Gregus for a long time and understand how the Lemoires felt when you oppressed them."

With these words, he threw the sunstone with force and broke it into many fragments.

Seeing this, the dragons bowed their heads to Arvin as one.

"For your wisdom and kindness, we will forever be in your debt," they answered, "We will never oppress the Lemoires and will live in peace with them!"

"Well," said Arvin, "then I will have one request for you. Help me return to the city of Yols, the city in the clouds."

"It will be an honour for us," the dragons replied.

Loy and Elma clapped their hands happily.

"How glad I am that you have become yourself again, my dear friend Yol!" Loy said and hugged him.

Elma smiled shyly.

"When you go on your next trip, take me with you!" he added.

"Aren't you afraid?" Arvin asked.

"There is no more fear in my heart," Loy replied, "but only a thirst for adventure."

Arvin smiled, about to head home, but Elma stopped him, inviting him to the castle.

Chapter 7

The Gift

"You can't leave just like that," said Elma. "There are many valuable things in the castle, brought from all over the world. Gregus didn't let anyone near them for years, but we owe you one. And for your exploits, you can choose whatever you like."

Arvin did not need anything, but he could not refuse Elma, who wanted to show her gratitude. Together, they descended into the depths of the castle, where there was a lot of gold, jewels and other objects.

"Take whatever you want," said Elma.

Arvin examined outlandish things of various forms, but among all this magnificence, a huge stone stood out, which sparkled so brightly that it illuminated the entire hall.

"What is it?" he asked Elma.

"This is the petrified heart of a dragon, the largest of all that the world has ever seen," she replied. "They say it can work miracles... but no one could move it from its place for many centuries. It is said that only one with a dragon heart will do this."

"That's exactly what I need," Arvin replied, taking it easily in his hands.

Now he knew how to thank the noble Ikhars.

Elma gasped. How beautiful, strong and smart this Yol seemed to her. She immediately offered to help him rule the kingdom of Dragon Island.

Arvin really wanted to stay and felt sad at the thought of having to leave this place. However, he remembered that he had to repay the noble Ikhars, see his family and tell the Yols about all he saw. He said goodbye to Elma and promised her to return.

Arvin climbed onto the back of the golden dragon. The dragon immediately took to the air. In less than a few hours, a city appeared in the distance in the sky among the clouds.

Only now, the young Yol realised how much he missed it.

The dragon landed right in the courtyard of the noble Ikhars' house. They immediately came out and surrounded them. With admiration and bated breath, they examined the dragon.

"I returned," said Arvin, "And brought you what you asked for."

He took out the petrified dragon heart and offered it to them.

The noble Ikhars took it in their hands. At that very moment, a miracle happened. The clouds surrounding the city of Yols parted, revealing many roads and endless views to the horizon.

Yols jumped out of their homes. Many of them climbed onto rooftops to see what had happened. They could not believe that there was something outside their city, and even more so that now all the roads to the world were open to them. They saw in the distance cities and countries that they did not even suspect existed. Now they had much to believe and much to learn.

"So, you managed to fall into the sky," said the noble Ikhars. "Now you are the greatest Yol of all. How proud we are of you!"

Arvin smiled.

"With this heart, you can create many new miracles."

But old Ikhar thought for a moment and then stepped forward.

"Now we see that this is too much to pay for our help."

"No," answered Arvin.

"Without you, I would never have got out of the city in the clouds. Take this petrified heart and use it for the good of our people."

"It will be an honour for us," answered the Ikhars. "We will no longer hide the secrets of our art but will begin to share them with the world."

Then he went home and embraced old Grokhan and the silent Ruzelda.

"How grateful I am to you, Mother, for your bracelet! It has rescued me more than once in distant lands! And your stories, Grandpa! All of them turned out to be true!"

They were so happy to see him! Ruzelda hugged him tightly and kissed him.

And Grandfather could not wait to hear about everything he saw and learned! Arvin, on the other hand, began to create a map of the heavens, but in order to complete it, he had to visit many more different places.

But that's another story!

Thank you for reading a book from our project and joining our journey in the Garden of Happy stories and adventures!
Audio books are also being introduced on our site.

Soon we will publish comics and prints of the main heroes from our stories!
Welcome!
Stay with us!

Books are published in both English and Russian.

Published books of
our project:

Zinaida Kirko

Zinaida Kirko

WELCOME TO
THE HAPPY STORY GARDEN

https//thehappystorygarden.co.uk